LEO TOLSTOY

Philipok

Patricia Lee Gauch, Editor

With special thanks to Gennady Spirin, Jr.,
for his original translation

Philomel Books, Reg. U.S. Pat. & Tm. Off. Published simultaneously in Canada.

Printed in Hong Kong by South China Printing Co. (1988) Ltd.

Book design by Gunta Alexander. The text is set in Arrus.

The illustrations were done in watercolor on Arches watercolor paper.

Library of Congress Cataloging-in-Publication Data

Beneduce, Ann Keay. Philipok / by Leo Tolstoy; retold by Ann Keay Beneduce
and illustrated by Gennady Spirin.   p. cm.

Summary: Philipok's mother has told him that he is too young to
go to school, but one day he sets out to go on his own.

[1. Schools—Fiction. 2. Russia—Fiction.] I. Tolstoy, Leo, graf, 1828-1910.

II. Spirin, Gennadii, ill. III. Title. PZ7.B432345 Ph 2000

[E]—dc21 99-055298   ISBN 0-399-23482-9

1 3 5 7 9 10 8 6 4 2

First Impression

LEO TOLSTOY

Philipok

Illustrated by
Gennady Spirin

Retold by
Ann Keay Beneduce

Philomel Books ♦ New York

There was once a boy named Philipok. One morning, when his big brother, Peter, went to school, Philipok put on his hat and started to follow him.

"Where are you off to, Philipok?" his mother asked.

"To school, like Peter."

"Oh, no, Philipok, you can't go. You're still too young. You stay here with Grandma."

And Mother went off to work. Father had already left for his job in the forest. Grandma sat by the warm stove, knitting, while Philipok played.

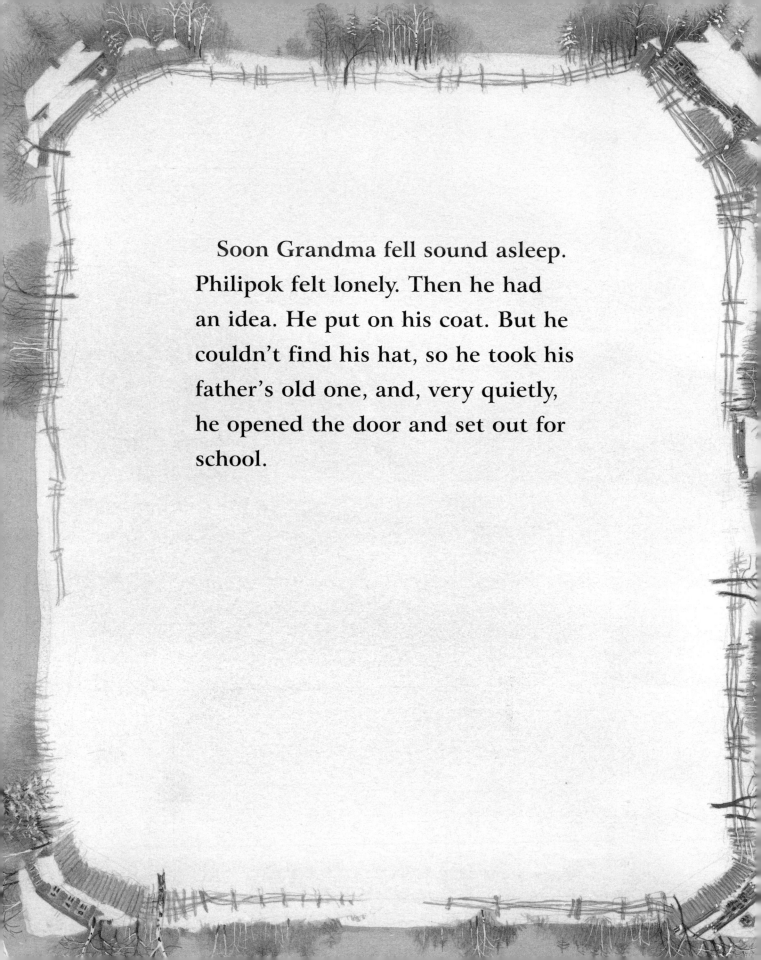

Soon Grandma fell sound asleep.
Philipok felt lonely. Then he had
an idea. He put on his coat. But he
couldn't find his hat, so he took his
father's old one, and, very quietly,
he opened the door and set out for
school.

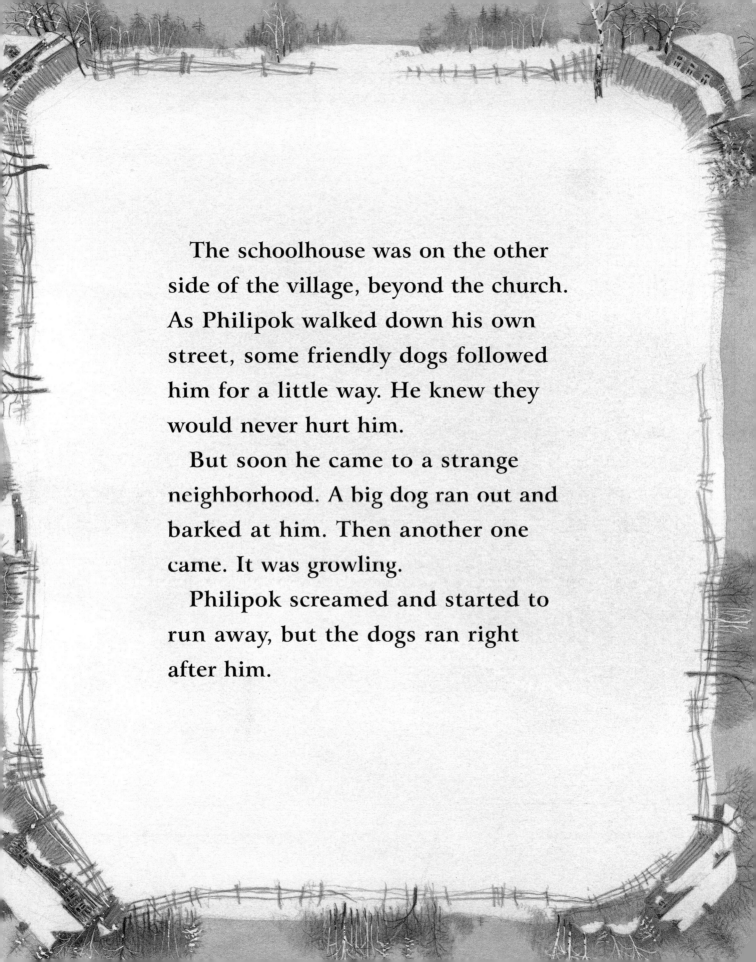

The schoolhouse was on the other side of the village, beyond the church. As Philipok walked down his own street, some friendly dogs followed him for a little way. He knew they would never hurt him.

But soon he came to a strange neighborhood. A big dog ran out and barked at him. Then another one came. It was growling.

Philipok screamed and started to run away, but the dogs ran right after him.

Philipok's foot slipped—he tripped
and fell down.

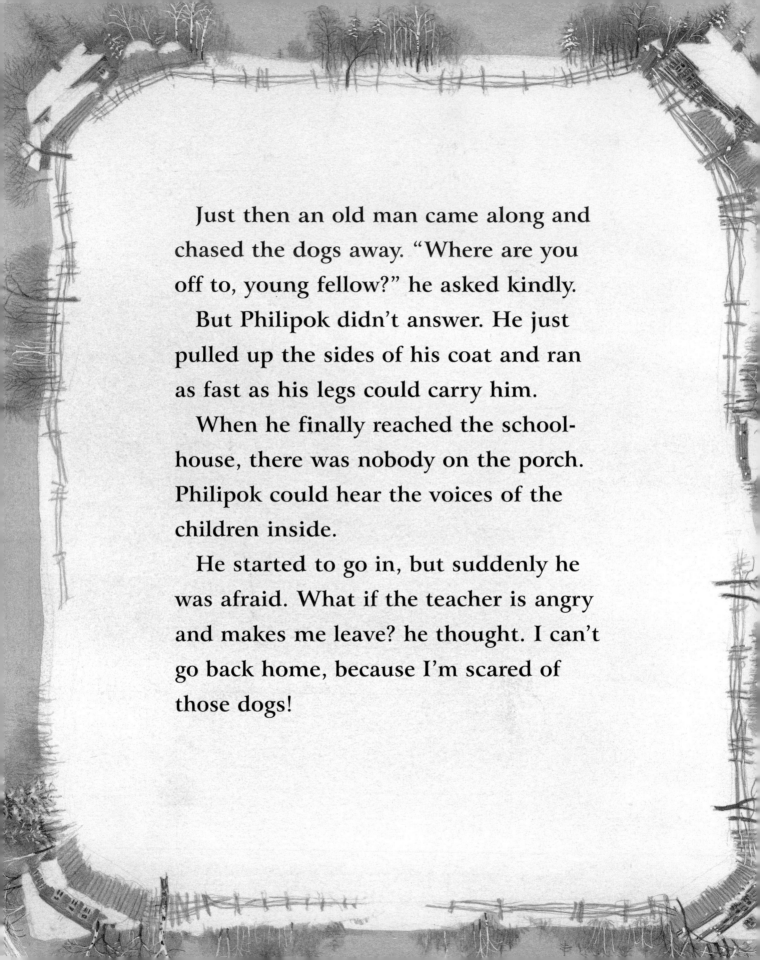

Just then an old man came along and chased the dogs away. "Where are you off to, young fellow?" he asked kindly.

But Philipok didn't answer. He just pulled up the sides of his coat and ran as fast as his legs could carry him.

When he finally reached the school-house, there was nobody on the porch. Philipok could hear the voices of the children inside.

He started to go in, but suddenly he was afraid. What if the teacher is angry and makes me leave? he thought. I can't go back home, because I'm scared of those dogs!

Then a woman carrying pails of water walked by. "What are you doing out here?" she demanded. "You should be inside studying with everyone else! You get right in there this minute!" Philipok quickly ducked into the schoolhouse.

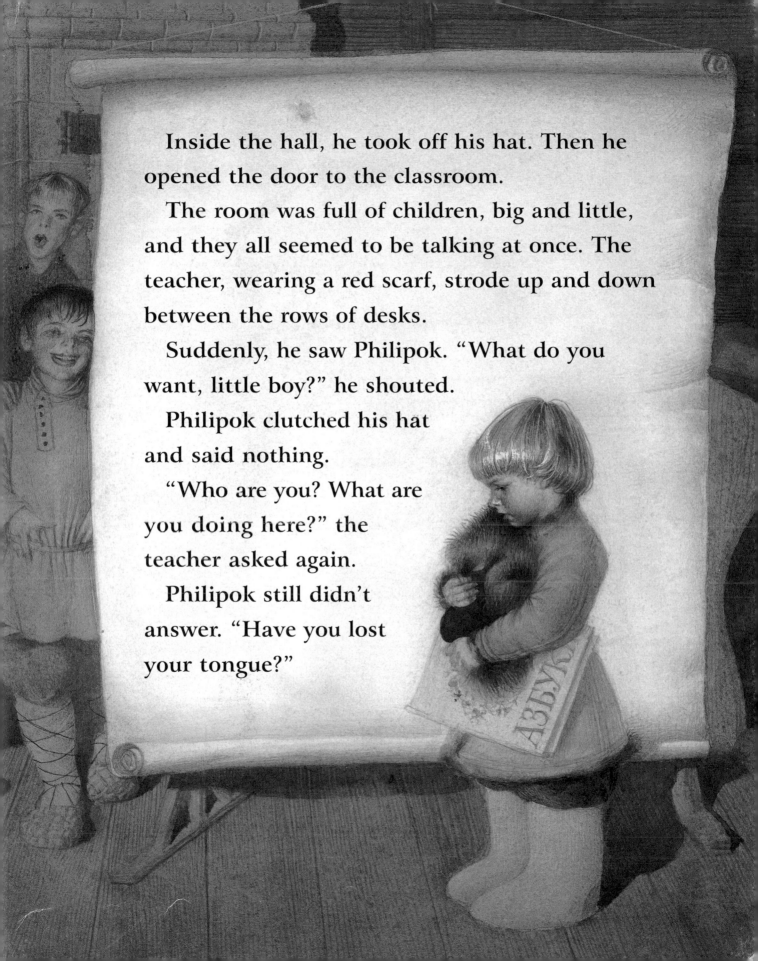

Inside the hall, he took off his hat. Then he opened the door to the classroom.

The room was full of children, big and little, and they all seemed to be talking at once. The teacher, wearing a red scarf, strode up and down between the rows of desks.

Suddenly, he saw Philipok. "What do you want, little boy?" he shouted.

Philipok clutched his hat and said nothing.

"Who are you? What are you doing here?" the teacher asked again.

Philipok still didn't answer. "Have you lost your tongue?"

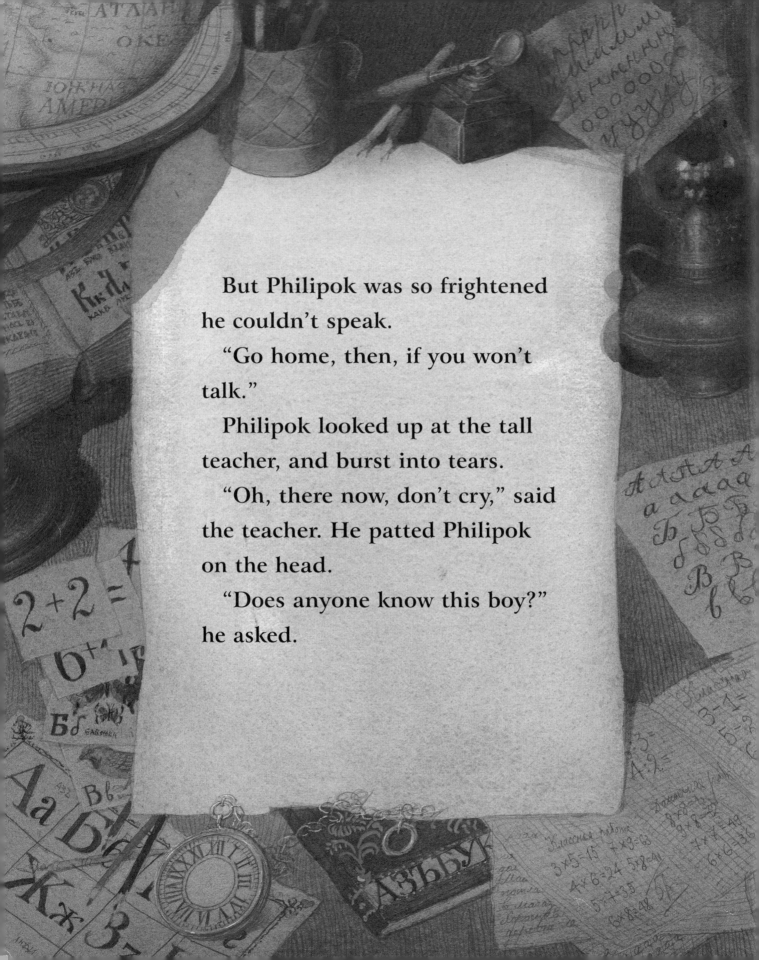

But Philipok was so frightened he couldn't speak.

"Go home, then, if you won't talk."

Philipok looked up at the tall teacher, and burst into tears.

"Oh, there now, don't cry," said the teacher. He patted Philipok on the head.

"Does anyone know this boy?" he asked.

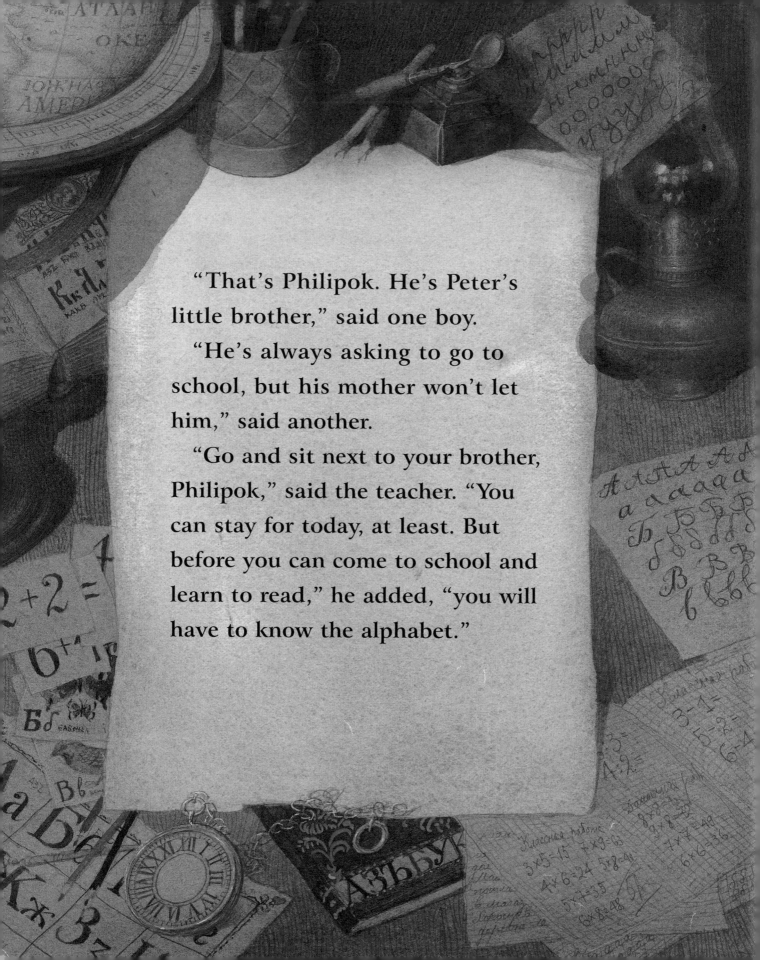

"That's Philipok. He's Peter's little brother," said one boy.

"He's always asking to go to school, but his mother won't let him," said another.

"Go and sit next to your brother, Philipok," said the teacher. "You can stay for today, at least. But before you can come to school and learn to read," he added, "you will have to know the alphabet."

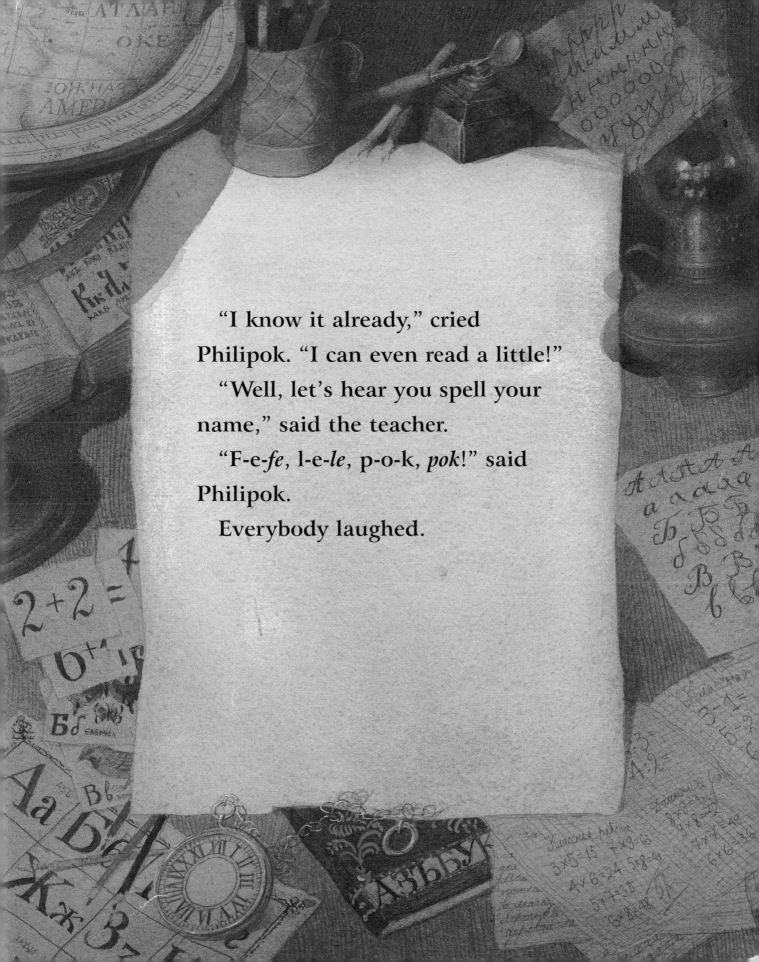

"I know it already," cried Philipok. "I can even read a little!"

"Well, let's hear you spell your name," said the teacher.

"F-e-*fe*, l-e-*le*, p-o-k, *pok*!" said Philipok.

Everybody laughed.

But the teacher said, "Good boy! Who has been teaching you?"

"Peter, my brother," answered Philipok. Then, feeling bolder, he went on, "I'm really clever: I learn very quickly. You see, I'm *very* smart!"

The teacher laughed. "You'd better stop bragging and start learning," he said. "I'll tell your mother you can come to school."

And so, after that, Philipok went happily
to school every day with his big brother, Peter,
and all the other children.

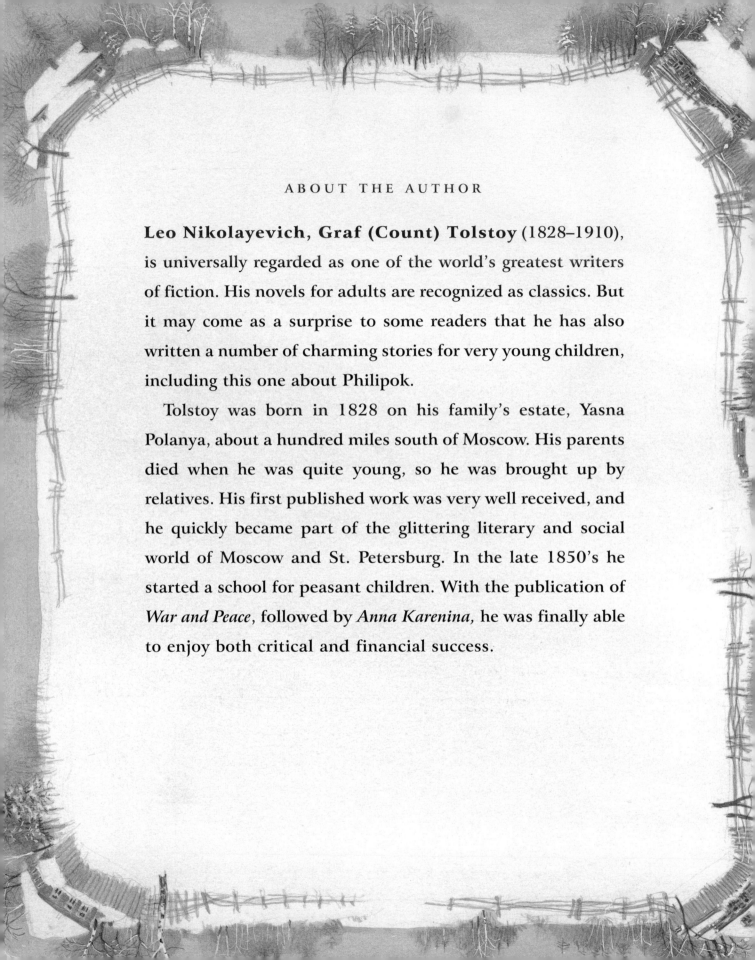

ABOUT THE AUTHOR

Leo Nikolayevich, Graf (Count) Tolstoy (1828–1910), is universally regarded as one of the world's greatest writers of fiction. His novels for adults are recognized as classics. But it may come as a surprise to some readers that he has also written a number of charming stories for very young children, including this one about Philipok.

Tolstoy was born in 1828 on his family's estate, Yasna Polanya, about a hundred miles south of Moscow. His parents died when he was quite young, so he was brought up by relatives. His first published work was very well received, and he quickly became part of the glittering literary and social world of Moscow and St. Petersburg. In the late 1850's he started a school for peasant children. With the publication of *War and Peace*, followed by *Anna Karenina,* he was finally able to enjoy both critical and financial success.

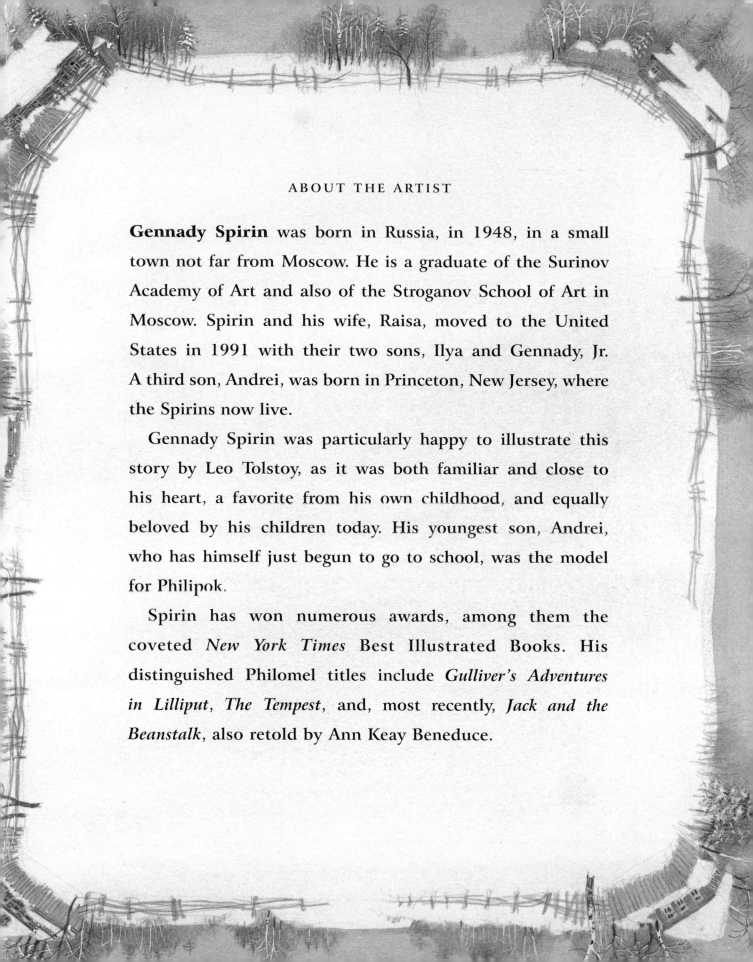

ABOUT THE ARTIST

Gennady Spirin was born in Russia, in 1948, in a small town not far from Moscow. He is a graduate of the Surinov Academy of Art and also of the Stroganov School of Art in Moscow. Spirin and his wife, Raisa, moved to the United States in 1991 with their two sons, Ilya and Gennady, Jr. A third son, Andrei, was born in Princeton, New Jersey, where the Spirins now live.

Gennady Spirin was particularly happy to illustrate this story by Leo Tolstoy, as it was both familiar and close to his heart, a favorite from his own childhood, and equally beloved by his children today. His youngest son, Andrei, who has himself just begun to go to school, was the model for Philipok.

Spirin has won numerous awards, among them the coveted *New York Times* Best Illustrated Books. His distinguished Philomel titles include *Gulliver's Adventures in Lilliput*, *The Tempest*, and, most recently, *Jack and the Beanstalk*, also retold by Ann Keay Beneduce.

ABOUT THE RETELLER

Ann Keay Beneduce, a former children's book editor, has written a number of books for children, including retellings of *Jack and the Beanstalk* and of William Shakespeare's *The Tempest,* as well as an adaptation of *Gulliver's Adventures in Lilliput* (Jonathan Swift), all illustrated by Gennady Spirin. In this book she has retold the story of Philipok in a simple, easy-to-read style, very similar to that employed by Tolstoy in his Russian original.